Ecosystems
Deserts

by Tim Mayerling

MW00837706

Bullfrog
Books

Ideas for Parents and Teachers

Bullfrog Books let children practice reading informational text at the earliest reading levels. Repetition, familiar words, and photo labels support early readers.

Before Reading

- Discuss the cover photo. What does it tell them?

- Look at the picture glossary together. Read and discuss the words.

Read the Book

- "Walk" through the book and look at the photos. Let the child ask questions. Point out the photo labels.

- Read the book to the child, or have him or her read independently.

After Reading

- Prompt the child to think more. Ask: Have you ever visited a desert? Have you seen videos or pictures? How would you describe it?

Bullfrog Books are published by Jump!
5357 Penn Avenue South
Minneapolis, MN 55419
www.jumplibrary.com

Copyright © 2018 Jump! International copyright reserved in all countries. No part of this book may be reproduced in any form without written permission from the publisher.

Library of Congress Cataloging-in-Publication Data

Names: Mayerling, Tim, author.
Title: Deserts / by Tim Mayerling.
Description: Minneapolis, MN: Jump!, Inc. [2017]*
Series: Ecosystems | Audience: Ages 5–8.
Audience: K to grade 3.
Includes bibliographical references and index.
Identifiers: LCCN 2016053481 (print)
LCCN 2016054962 (ebook)
ISBN 9781620316771 (hardcover: alk. paper)
ISBN 9781620317303 (pbk.)
ISBN 9781624965548 (ebook)
Subjects: LCSH: Desert ecology—Juvenile literature.
Deserts—Juvenile literature.
Classification: LCC QH541.5.D4 M394 2017 (print)
LCC QH541.5.D4 (ebook) | DDC 577.54—dc23
LC record available at https://lccn.loc.gov/2016053481

Editor: Jenny Fretland VanVoorst
Book Designer: Molly Ballanger
Photo Researcher: Molly Ballanger

Photo Credits: Alamy: Jose B. Ruiz, 10–11; Jack Goldfarb, 18–19; Andrea Battisti, 20–21. Getty: Auscape, 17. iStock: idizimage, 5. Shutterstock: Chad Zuber, cover; Natalia van D, 1; Marijane Troche, 3; elleon, 4; saraporn, 6–7; Anton Foltin, 8–9, 12; aleksandr hunta, 13; Stefan Scharf, 14–15; Zhiltsov Alexandr, 16; EcoPrint, 20–21; Eric Isselee, 24.

Printed in the United States of America at Corporate Graphics in North Mankato, Minnesota.

Table of Contents

Hot, Cold, and Dry

A desert is a dry place.

It does not rain often.

Look! The ground is dry.

It is cracked.

Deserts are found all over the world.

Some are cold.

But most are hot.

A desert is a harsh place.

How do living things survive?

They adapt.
Plants store water
in their stems.

Some have small leaves.
Others have none at all.

leaves

Animals adapt, too.

Most desert animals are small.

Why?

They do not need as much food.

Index

To Learn More

Learning more is as easy as 1, 2, 3.

1) Go to www.factsurfer.com

2) Enter "deserts" into the search box.

3) Click the "Surf" button to see a list of websites.

With factsurfer.com, finding more information is just a click away.

Picture Glossary

adapt
To change in order to fit a particular situation.

harsh
Making many or difficult demands.

cold-blooded
Having a body temperature not regulated by the body and close to that of the environment.

survive
To live.

They rest during the day.

They come out at night.

It is cooler then.

17

Some are cold-blooded.
They need the desert's
heat to keep warm.

A desert is a
harsh place.

But it is full of life!

Where Are the Deserts?

Most deserts are hot during the day and cold at night. Some deserts, though, are cold all the time. They are in Antarctica and at higher elevations.

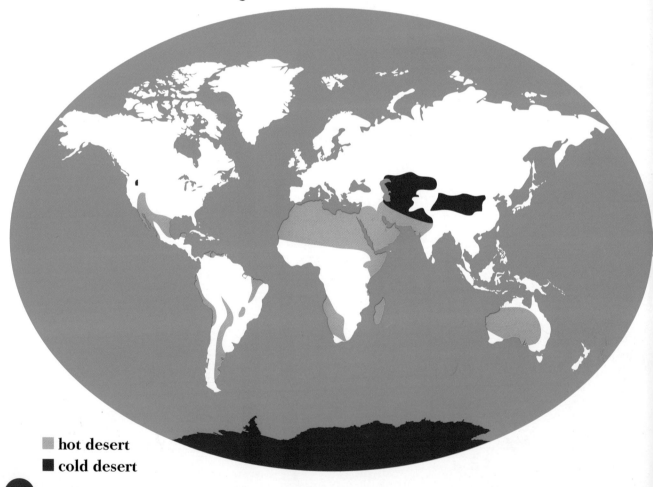

■ hot desert
■ cold desert

index

Ready to Learn More?

 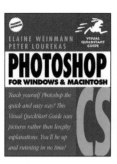   

If you enjoyed this project and are ready to learn more, pick up a *Visual QuickStart Guide*, the best-selling, most affordable, most trusted, quick-reference series for computing.

With more than 5.5 million copies in print, *Visual QuickStart Guides* are the industry's best-selling series of affordable, quick-reference guides. This series from Peachpit Press includes more than 200 titles covering the leading applications for digital photography and illustration, digital video and sound editing, Web design and development, business productivity, graphic design, operating systems, and more. Best of all, these books respect your time and intelligence. With tons of well-chosen illustrations and practical, labor-saving tips, they'll have you up to speed on new software fast.

> *"When you need to quickly learn to use a new application or new version of an application, you can't do better than the **Visual QuickStart Guides** from Peachpit Press."*
> Jay Nelson
> *Design Tools Monthly*

www.peachpit.com